D1633961

The Rajah was out hunting on his elephant. He was hunting tigers.

The Rajah's elephant was painted in purple and ochre and vermilion. It was hung with velvet and jewels and tasselled with silk. The Rajah's elephant had a telephone and a bar and a new stereo tape cassette player. The Rajah talked to his office on the telephone and he listened to light classics on his new stereo tape cassette player.

In a rack within easy reach were the Rajah's monogrammed gold-mounted jewelled tiger guns. Many rounds of ammunition were in boxes inlaid with ivory and mother-of-pearl at his feet. A servant stood by in the gilded howdah ready to reload the guns as fast as the Rajah could fire them while another servant mixed drinks at the bar. Trackers and beaters went through the jungle ahead and behind.

The tigers had no stereo tape cassette players and no telephones. They didn't wear shoes, they were primitive. They had no guns, whenever they killed anything they got all bloody.

Ah, but they could dance! Nobody danced like the tigers, nobody could even think of such dances as they did. Moon dances, shadow dances, silence dances and dances for the starlight and the glimmers on the river. Even the child tigers among them danced the most complex patterns and difficult rhythms in the bending grasses and the shadows of the jungle under the hissing and humming of the moon, under the racing clouds, under the teeming rain.

Nobody knew of their dancing, nobody had ever heard of it or imagined such a thing, and the tigers held their tongues. Silently prowling in their stripes they hunted, unseen they roared and started sudden echoes. They knew they would be hunted down, they knew that every season some of them would die by a bullet from the Rajah's monogrammed gold-mounted jewelled tiger guns. They were primitive and patient and they accepted their lot.

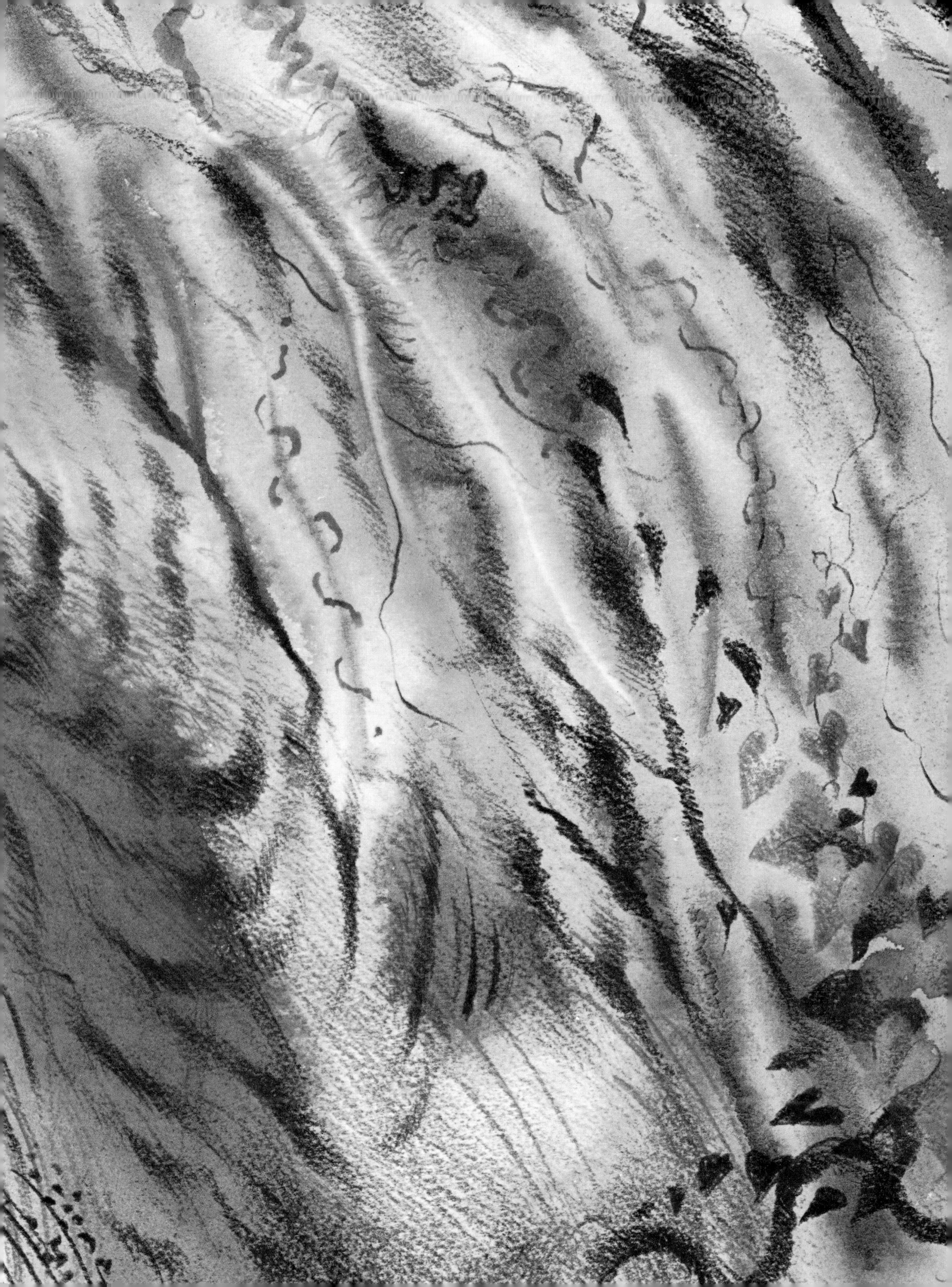

When the Rajah came into the jungle on his elephant there was sorrow among the tigers. Families huddled together cursing and praying by turns. Fathers and mothers wept over their children soon to be orphans. There was nowhere to escape to, only other jungles and other Rajahs. The tigers had little to hope for. They posted sentries and they waited.

From the outposts came the word that the Rajah on his elephant was coming closer. The tigers cursed and prayed and waited.

From the outposts came the word that the Rajah had a new stereo tape cassette player on which he played light classics.

"What are light classics?" said one of the tiger elders. His question was relayed to the outposts.

"You will know them when you hear them," came the answer. "Only light classics have the sound of light classics."

The tigers waited. The elder said, "This too may perhaps be borne. If it is our fate to be killed by the Rajah then die we must. Perhaps he sees the tragedy of the thing. Perhaps he is saddened that all unknowing he stills our dancing that he has never seen and is not even capable of imagining. Perhaps he senses this and does us honour in this fashion."

Then they heard the cries of birds that flew up from the trees as the Rajah came through the jungle on his elephant that was painted purple and ochre and vermilion. From the new stereo tape cassette player they heard the blare of music in the dappled sunlight and deep shadow of the jungle. It was Hippolytov-Ivanov's *Caucasian Sketches*.

"What the deuce is that?" said all the tigers.

"That's light classics," said the elder. "There's no mistaking it. I'll tell you what this is, it's simply too much. It's one thing to accept one's fate but it's quite another thing to perish with light classics shattering the stillness. It's insulting. It's degrading."

"Hear, hear!" shouted most of the tigers. Very few hung back.

"Now listen to me," said the elder. "My whole world-picture has suddenly changed. As long as the Rajah knew his place it seemed to me that I knew mine but now I can't think how I could have been such a fool. I'll tell you what I'm thinking."

"What?" said all the tigers.

"I'm thinking of dancing him to death," said the elder. "Him and his trackers and his beaters, his mahout and his servants, the whole ruddy lot of them."

"Well, there it is," said all the tigers. "Why not? It's certainly no worse than hanging about and being shot down."

The tigers stopped praying and they stopped cursing. In what little time they had until the beaters were upon them they quickly decided who should dance what. Then they wished one another luck and got on with it. They didn't wait to hear the gongs and shouts of the beaters, they called for volunteers and sent the first one out to dance. They counted heavily on the element of surprise.

The Rajah had his rifle at the ready. He expected to see a running tiger, he did not expect a dancing one. He did not fire immediately. The first tiger volunteer was a female, cool and brave and elegant. She fixed her amber eyes upon the Rajah and she wove herself into and out of the shadows as she danced the stillness of the jungle that waits.

"Ah!" said the Rajah, "There never was such dancing!" He shut off the stereo tape cassette player so he could see it better.

"Better not watch," said his mahout. "You'll be sorry if you do."

"I've never seen the like," the Rajah said. "I'd no idea that tigers were up to this sort of thing." He laid down his rifle, leant his chin on his hand and watched.

While the first tiger was still dancing a second one came out to join her. A powerful male, he danced the terror of the jungle that is partner to the stillness. The Rajah was enchanted.

"Primitive they may be," he said, "but they've got something, they really have."

"Tell you what," said the mahout. "I'd like to put this elephant in reverse and clear out of here."

"No, indeed," the Rajah said. "I feel as if I've waited all my life for this. It must have been the music that got them started. It's quite amazing, really. I shall write a letter to *The Times* about this."

The Rajah watched, the tigers danced, other tigers one by one came from the shadows dancing.

The sun went down, the moon rose over the dancing tigers and the Rajah watched while the mahout shivered and hid his face.

The night wore on and all the tigers danced now, old and young, the grown ones and the children. They danced the moon dance and the shadow dance and the dance for the starlight and the glimmers on the river. Under the hissing and the humming of the moon, under the racing clouds they danced. They danced the moon down low and pale into the morning. Some perhaps were moved to pity but they could not stop. The dance was in them and they danced it.

In the dawn the birds sang the morning stillness into day but the Rajah never heard them. Nor his mahout nor his servants and his trackers and his beaters.

The Rajah still leant his chin on his hand but as the elephant turned and walked back out of the jungle he fell forward. His head struck the PLAY button of the stereo tape cassette player and he rode back to his palace dead while the swaying elephant alone heard the *Caucasian Sketches* of Hippolytov-Ivanov.

In the dawn the birds sang the morning stillness into day but the Rajah never heard them. Nor his mahout nor his servants and his trackers and his beaters.

The Rajah still leant his chin on his hand but as the elephant turned and walked back out of the jungle he fell forward. His head struck the PLAY button of the stereo tape cassette player and he rode back to his palace dead while the swaying elephant alone heard the *Caucasian Sketches* of Hippolytov-Ivanov.

First published 1979

Jonathan Cape Ltd, 30 Bedford Square, London WC1

British Library Cataloguing in Publication Data

Hoban, Russell
The dancing tigers.
1. Children's stories, English
I. Title   II. Gentleman, David
823'.9'1J   PZ8.9H6/

ISBN 0-224-01374-2

Printed and bound in Great Britain by
Morrison & Gibb Ltd, London and Edinburgh